ZANE'S NINJA TRAINING MANUAL

YOUR STEP-BY-STEP GUIDE TO BECOMING A SPINJITZU NINJA

By Meredith Rusu

Scholastic Inc.

Published by Scholastic Inc., *Publishers since 1920.* SCHOLASTIC and associated logos are trademarks and/ or registered trademarks of Scholastic Inc.

The publisher does not have any control over and does not assume any responsibility for author or third-party websites or their content.

This book is a work of fiction. Names, characters, places, and incidents are either the product of the author's imagination or are used fictitiously, and any resemblance to actual persons, living or dead, business establishments, events, or locales is entirely coincidental.

ISBN 978-1-338-16279-0

10 9 8 7 6 5 4 3 2 1   17 18 19 20 21

Printed in China   68

First printing 2017

ZANE'S NINJA TRAINING MANUAL

YOUR STEP-BY-STEP GUIDE TO BECOMING A SPINJITZU NINJA

INTRODUCTION

Greetings. My name is Zane, and I am a ninja. If you have picked up this manual, it means you desire to unlock your true potential. I am here to help you achieve that goal.

Becoming a ninja is not easy. It takes years of hard work and training. To rush unprepared into battle against, say, the Digital Overlord would be . . . unadvisable. This guide will provide the building blocks you need to begin your journey.

You may have noticed that I am a Nindroid. One of the most important lessons you will discover in this book is that our differences make up our greatest strengths. I learned that from Master Wu, my teacher. His wisdom helped make me the ninja I am today. Now it is my turn to pass his lessons on to you.

WHAT IS A SPINJITZU NINJA?

A Spinjitzu ninja is someone who protects those who can't protect themselves. Ninja are loyal, honest, and courageous. We work together to help friends and family. Above all, ninja never quit!

According to my databanks, there are five core values you must master to become a ninja:

Nerve	Be courageous and never give up in the face of adversity.
Integrity	Always be honest and true to your team.
k**N**owledge	Work hard, study, and don't be afraid of hard work.
Judgment	Use sound judgment to face every problem.
Action	Know when it is time to act!

ZANE'S WISDOM

Some ninja are elemental masters. This means we can control natural forces such as water, energy, and ice. As a ninja-in-training, you must discover your own element to master.

An element can be anything: knowledge, music, or even games. My friend Jay insists he can control the element of humor. People do find him funny. Perhaps he is correct.

I am the Titanium Ninja. I have trained for years under Master Wu with my fellow ninja, Kai, Cole, Jay, Lloyd, and Nya. They are more than just my team — they are my family.

Here are some of the most important things they have taught me:

Trust in your team: Working together, you can overcome any enemy.

Be yourself: Believe in yourself, no matter how different you seem. Each individual is unique. You may not master the same moves as your friends, and that is as it should be. Your Spinjitzu will reflect the qualities and strength that are special to you.

Face your fears: Each of us has obstacles and worries that can hold us back from true greatness. You must conquer those fears to set your heart free.

Make time for fun: My friends helped me find my "humor" switch. It was . . . illuminating.

Never stop learning: Spinjitzu is a lifelong journey. Even Master Wu is still a student of Spinjitzu! Your potential is greater than you can even imagine.

ZANE SAYS:

My friends often use words of inspiration to "pump themselves up" in times of trouble. Here are some of my "catchy quotes." My friends tell me they have found these quite useful. Many of them are inspired by the lessons I have learned from Master Wu.

"A NINJA **NEVER** LEAVES ANOTHER NINJA'S SIDE."

"I GUESS IT'S TRUE; THE PATH WE SEEK IS NEVER A STRAIGHT LINE."

"NO ONE EVER SAID BEING A **HERO** WAS EASY. ALTHOUGH OUR **GOOD DEEDS** MAY NEVER MAKE US RICH, THEY MAKE US RICH IN OTHER WAYS."

"WE ALL MAY HAVE DIFFERENT BACKGROUNDS, BUT WE ALL SHARE THE SAME FUTURE."

STRONGER TOGETHER

The only way to become a ninja is to work with your team. Each of my friends has followed his or her own path, yet we have all helped one another unlock our true potential. Your friends can help you unlock your true potential, too.

Pixal: Pixal was a Nindroid before an enemy destroyed her mechanics. To save her, I placed her memory chip in my own neural drive. Now we are truly compatible.

Master Wu
Our mentor

Jay
Lightning Ninja

Lloyd
Green Ninja

Kai
Fire Ninja

Nya
Water Ninja

Cole
Earth Ninja

Zane
Titanium Ninja

KAI'S WISDOM

Kai is all about action. He kicks our team into high gear when we need to get going. Kai has taught me that actions can speak louder than words, and you should always give 100 percent of yourself to any challenge.

Kai and Nya are brother and sister. Just as water tempers fire, Kai's hot-headedness is kept in check by his sister's logic . . . and humor!

Kai's energy drives our team.

Kai says: "A ninja never accepts defeat. A ninja always picks himself up when he's down."

COLE'S WISDOM

Cole is very grounded. I can always trust him for sound judgment. As a ninja-in-training, it is important for you to ground yourself in the here and now. Do not waste time worrying about what you cannot change; focus on what you can.

Cole insists on having a solid plan before squaring off against an enemy.

Cole was once a ghost. But the friendship of his fellow ninja kept him grounded in the living world. He has taught me many things: loyalty, leadership, and trust.

Cole says: "A ninja doesn't save himself — he protects those who cannot protect themselves."

NYA'S WISDOM

Nya is strong-willed and resourceful. She has taught me about determination in the face of insurmountable odds. Her knowledge of technology is also impressive. (Coming from a Nindroid, that means a lot!)

Nya says: "If you want something bad enough, you find a way to make it happen."

Before she was a ninja, Nya created the Samurai X armor to fight in secret. It was quite ingenious!

Nya is the Elemental Master of Water. Her determination to unlock her true potential reminded me what being a ninja is all about.

JAY'S WISDOM

Jay is very inventive. He sees solutions to problems that others cannot. He also has an excellent sense of humor, or so he tells me. I look to Jay to see the funny side of things.

Jay's jokes help us get through tough times. The team that laughs together is stronger together.

Jay says: "Let's chop-socky this lemonade stand!"

As the Master of Lightning, Jay is not only shockingly funny. He is shockingly powerful, too.

LLOYD'S WISDOM

Lloyd is our team leader and Master-in-Training. I have been able to count on him for sound advice many times. From Lloyd, I have learned that there is always room to grow.

Lloyd aspires to be a wise teacher like his uncle, Master Wu.

Lloyd has been shouldered with great power as the prophesied Green Ninja. Out of all of us, he has been required to grow the most in the least amount of time.

Lloyd says: "We fight for each other. We fight as one."

MASTER WU'S WISDOM

Master Wu trained all of us to become Spinjitzu ninja. He taught me that Spinjitzu revolves around balance. To become a true ninja, your body and mind must be balanced. A ninja must achieve this balance to become a Spinjitzu master.

Master Wu helped me realize that I just needed to be myself, circuits and all, to unlock my true potential. He also taught me to appreciate tea (even though I never drink it).

Master Wu seems to know what we need to do before we realize it ourselves. He always encourages us to be our best.

Master Wu says: "A true ninja can see what others do not."

A NINJA'S GREATEST CHALLENGE

As a ninja-in-training, you will face many trials. Here are some of the most difficult times my friends and I have faced as ninja.

Kai secretly hoped that *he* would become the powerful Green Ninja. When he discovered Lloyd was the Green Ninja, Kai had to face the disappoint-  ment that his dream would never come true. In the end, he grew even stronger as the Fire Ninja, realizing that was his destiny.

When we fought the Time Twins, we needed a leader to help us face the challenge. Lloyd became that leader. He had to learn when to trust his own wisdom — and when to listen to his team. He learned from his mistakes and became a true master.

Nya has always been a key member of our ninja team. And for a while, she fought solo as the original Samurai X. Her greatest challenge came when she discovered she, too, had an elemental power. She tapped into her true potential and became the Water Ninja.

NINJA GADGETS

A well-stocked supply of gadgets is a great asset to a ninja. As a ninja, you will come across gadgets, weapons, and artifacts that can be both useful and highly dangerous. Here are some of the most powerful weapons my friends and I have encountered during our journeys.

TECHNO BLADES: The Techno Blades can "hack" into any technological system and take over it, giving the holder digital control over reality.

TIME BLADES: Each of the Time Blades gives the holder a specific power over time. One blade can speed time up, another can reverse it, and one can even stop time in its tracks.

GOLDEN WEAPONS: Our team used the Sword of Fire, the Nunchuks of Lightning, the Shurikens of Ice, and the Scythe of Quakes to battle enemies before the weapons were combined into the Mega Weapon.

SAMURAI X ARMOR: Nya invented the Samurai X armor in order to fight enemies before she discovered she was the Elemental Master of Water. It was quite an impressive battle suit!

REALM CRYSTAL: The Realm Crystal is a powerful stone that can open the

portal between Ninjago's realms. Though not exactly a gadget, it is potentially one of the most destructive artifacts we have ever encountered.

A NINJA'S GREATEST ENEMY

You will face many different types of enemies during your ninja training. Some enemies can be defeated easily. Others are . . . more troublesome. Some can even become allies.

THE GOOD

One of a ninja's greatest accomplishments is turning an enemy into an ally. Anyone can fight, but it takes true wisdom and courage to make your enemy your friend.

SKYLOR: Skylor is the daughter of the notorious Master Chen, and she is also the Elemental Master of Amber. That means she can absorb other's powers. At first, she battled alongside her father. But when we showed her the danger Chen's Anacondrai army posed to the Realms, she joined our side and helped us defeat him.

MASTER YANG: Trapped in the Temple of the Airjitzu for centuries, Master Yang's spirit was vengeful. But Cole helped him to realize that he was honored by all as the creator of Airjitzu. Now it appears Master Yang's spirit has been freed from his cursed fate.

RONIN: This master thief is cunning. He once hunted us down one by one. Yet his intentions were good. He thought we were criminals. And in times of great need, he has helped our team. My systems cannot compute a logical rationale for his behavior, but I believe this is one of those human instances of "irony."

THE "NOT-SO-BADDIES"

These are the enemies I would classify as "manageable." Jay calls them the "not-so-baddies." I believe Jay's reference is a joke, though it is certainly accurate.

PYTHOR: The last existing member of the ancient Anacondrai race of snakes, Pythor fought against us . . . then with us . . . then against us again. He has flipped sides so often, my internal processor cannot classify him as a friend or foe. Perhaps we can simply say he is "complex."

THE SKULKIN: The skeleton warriors were the first enemies we faced. At the time, they seemed powerful. But given the enemies our team has since encountered, they seem more "boneheaded."

NINDROIDS: Cyrus Borg invented the Nindroids to serve and repair New Ninjago City. But when the Digital Overlord hacked their systems and took control over them, the Nindroids became much more sinister. I took a personal interest in helping my friends defeat these droids gone bad.

THE BAD

Some enemies will stretch you to your limit. These are the more sinister foes you will face as a ninja. You will need to work closely with your team in order to defeat them.

THE TIME TWINS:

Perhaps two of the most fiendish enemies we have come across, Krux and Acronix laid in wait for forty years to finish their battle against the Elemental Masters. Krux disguised himself as Dr. Sander Saunders and worked for many years at the Ninjago Museum of History before his brother, Acronix, returned to help him seize power. Kai and Nya worked together as brother and sister to finish the fight that Wu and Garmadon began decades ago.

MASTER CHEN: Master Chen took me prisoner and used me to lure the other ninja to his deadly Tournament of Elements. Though he intended to divide us and steal our elemental powers, his efforts only united us further as a team.

THE GHOST WARRIORS:

Before it was destroyed, the Cursed Realm was home to many spiteful spirits just waiting for a chance to be released and take revenge. Our team had to band together and help Nya unlock her true potential as the Water Ninja in order to defeat these foes.

THE VERY, VERY BAD

Then there are the enemies that can only be defeated at great personal sacrifice. It is at times like these when, as a ninja, you must choose the good of the team over the good of the individual.

THE ANACONDRAI:

Once Master Chen had raised his new army of Anacondrai Warriors, it looked like all hope was lost. The only way to defeat the Anacondrai was to send them to the Cursed Realm.

THE DIGITAL OVERLORD: By combining the ancient Golden Powers with modern technology, the Digital Overlord sought to plunge Ninjago City into cyber darkness for eternity. In our final battle against him, I realized that the only thing that could destroy the Digital Overlord was an icy blast achieved by detonating my own power source. I did not want to leave my friends, but I had to protect them. Somehow, my memory banks were preserved, and I was rebuilt. I became the Titanium Ninja.

A NINJA'S LIFE

Of course, being a ninja is not all about battling enemies. It's about being there for your friends, doing good for the people around you, and, at times, playing a video game tournament or two.

HOME BASE: My friends and I have called many places home during our training. First was Master Wu's monastery, then the flying ship called *Destiny's Bounty*. Now we  train at the Temple of Airjitzu. I have learned it is important to have a place to call "home."

DARETH'S MOJO DOJO: Sometimes being a ninja means working with people who are a bit . . . unusual. We first met our friend Dareth when we needed to train Lloyd at Dareth's Mojo Dojo. Since then, Dareth has sort of . . . stuck around. On occasion, he has even helped us save the day! I do not understand his insistence that he is the "Brown Ninja." But for the sake of courtesy, I do not dispute it.

MASTER CHEN'S NOODLE HOUSE: My friends and I enjoy eating as a team at Master Chen's Noodle House. Though Master Chen was evil, he also made excellent noodles and puffy pot stickers. Since his defeat, Skylor has taken over the noodle shop, and my friends and I have been able to resume our team dinners.

A DAY IN THE LIFE OF A NINJA

6:00 AM: Wake up with the sunrise. Greet the day knowing there is much work to do.

7:00 AM: Team breakfast.

8:00 AM: Morning training. Remember to destroy *all* the targets.

11:00 AM: Daily errands; tea shopping. A ninja can never have enough tea, or so Master Wu says.

12:00 PM: Lunchtime. Time for some noodles!

1:30 PM: Repair tools and armor. Work on new inventions.

4:00 PM: Jay's Video Game Tournament (Round 75)

6:00 PM: Team dinner at Master Chen's Noodle House

7:30 PM: Outdoor night stealth training.

10:00 PM: Lights (and power switches) out.

NINJA HUMOR

Though my Nindroid sense of humor requires continual improvement, I have amassed an impressive memory bank of ninja jokes. Many are from Jay, some are from Kai and Cole, and some are even from Dareth. But they are all 100 percent ninja.

WHERE DID THE NINJA GET FOOD FOR HIS MISSION?

AT THE *STEALTH* FOOD STORE.

WHAT ARE A NINJA'S FAVORITE SHOES?

SNEAKERS

WHAT'S A NINJA'S FAVORITE DRINK?

KARA-*TEA*!

WHAT DO YOU GET WHEN YOU CROSS A PIG WITH A NINJA?

A PORK CHOP!

WHAT DID ONE NINJA SAY WHEN THE OTHER NINJA ASKED IF HE COULD TOSS HIM A THROWING STAR?

SHUR-I-KEN!

HOW DO YOU GIVE A NINJA DIREC-TIONS?

DON'T WORRY. HE'LL FIND YOU!

TRAINING COMPLETE

This brings us to the end of your ninja-in-training manual. There is a long road ahead of you to become a full ninja. But with the lessons you have learned, you will be on your way to fulfilling your destiny and unlocking your true potential. As Master Wu has taught me . . .

"THE PAST IS THE PAST, THE FUTURE IS YET TO COME. WE MUST MAKE THE MOST OF TODAY."

END OF MANUAL

Please proceed to the ninja-in-training activitie to further sharpen your skills.